Searching for Glisten, The Fairhope Dragon

Story by Debby Hackbarth
Illustrations by Carter Hlavin, Debby Hackbarth, and Jonah Hackbarth

1

Published by:
Intellect Publishing, LLC
www.IntellectPublishing.com

Visit the website: www.TheFairhopeDragonBook.com

Dedication:

To my husband, Jim, for his love, daily encouragement, and advice.

To my grandchildren, Katarina, Jonah, Carter, and Kaleb for their strength of character.

To my mother, Lucille (Lucy) and my grandmother Ruby for their intelligence and talent.

Thanks:

To Carter and Jonah for their extremely talented artwork.

To Bekah, Katarina, Carter, and Jim for their editing assistance.

To Tom Jones for his permission to highlight his talent and studio.

To the lovely city of Summerdale for permission to use their emblem.

Searching for Glisten,
The Fairhope Dragon

Ruby, William, and their teens: Jonah (16), Lucy (15), and Carter (14), inherited a farm from Ruby's parents, close to where Katarina and Kaleb lived on the Fish River. Ruby and William were excited to be able to home-school their children in a rural setting.

Mariposa met Ruby when they taught together at Fairhope High School. The ladies communicated for many years and Ruby knew about the twins and Mariposa's plan to leave the area with Glisten. Recently, Mariposa talked to the twins about Ruby's family. Kaleb and Katarina were anxious to meet Ruby and her family.

The twins were still sad about losing their cherished pet dragon, Glisten, and their guardian, Mariposa. They wanted to make plans to further their education and to find Glisten. William asked his children to bring Kaleb and Katarina to their home so all seven could discuss their future together.

Ruby included the twins in the family's home school. She organized a project schedule of twelve hours per week to coordinate and carry out a search for Glisten and Mariposa. She realized farm chores, preparing goods for sale at their roadside stands, and continued discoveries could alter the schedule.

Kaleb, Katarina, and Ruby's family planned to investigate the areas between their farms, the Weeks Bay National Estuarine Research Reserve, and Summerdale because Glisten took off in a northeast direction. The group knew they could not enter the reserve and they needed permission to hike on private property.

The seven explorers would use their many talents. William, a cartographer, taught Jonah map skills. Kaleb made walking sticks. Lucy and Ruby prepared delicious snacks. Katarina expertly sewed jackets and backpacks. Carter used his superb sense of direction to track animals.

For the upcoming trips to search
for Mariposa and Glisten, Katarina
supplied seven backpacks with
water Lucy delivered, tracking
journals Carter furnished, and
safety equipment that William
provided. Kaleb had walking
sticks for anyone who wanted one.

On their first quest, the group headed to Clay City to meet with William's friend, Tom. Since Tom worked locally, he could identify safe areas where Glisten might hide. Tom contacted friends to get permission for the adventurers to hike through their land legally.

After lunch, Lucy and Katarina visited the store, pet the dogs, and examined the iconic orange and tan tile that made Clay City famous. Carter, Kaleb, and Jonah admired the "bee hive" kiln and the pot forming machine.

The hikers explored the Clay City area for hours before returning home to take care of the animals. A few weeks later the quest began again because the families needed to take care of the farms and sell their goods. Kaleb could not wait to see the Navy Outlying Landing Field or NOLF on the east side of Summerdale.

On the Summerdale quest, Lucy, Katarina, and Ruby kept spirits up by singing, when the hikers became weary. William welcomed a chat with a couple who walked by. Jonah told the pair they were searching for a large flying creature. The twosome said they saw a huge animal flying southeast about a month earlier.

The following morning, Kaleb found a vase in their small barn while he took care of Bovine, his favorite cow. A tiny note was inside the vase. Katarina wanted to read the message during home school. When home school started the next day, she opened the note.

The message read:

My precious twins. Glisten and I
are headed for Wolf Bay because I
heard a dragon community may
be in that area. It's more difficult to
fly with each passing month, so I
decided to go now. Recently, I
sold my farm to Ruby and William
because I trust them and they
have funds to take care of you.
Please know I love you very much.
Ruby and William will care for you
as if you were their own children. I
hope you find Glisten and me
someday. Love, Mariposa

When a school break occurred, Ruby and Katarina contacted landowners west of Wolf Bay so the hikers could travel there legally. William, Kaleb, and Jonah organized the tents and sleeping equipment. Lucy and Carter prepared meals, snacks, and beverages for the group to enjoy for a few days. Ruby hired friends to take care of the two farms.

The next day, the enthusiastic explorers drove to the area where they planned to camp. After they set up camp, they headed out on the journey. Carter noted the Wolf Bay area was an ideal place for dragons to live because it was basically uninhabited. They hiked for a few hours and returned to the campsite.

Later, Kaleb heard a familiar sound and thought it might be Glisten. Sure enough, in a clearing, Katarina spotted Mariposa and Glisten. The twins rushed to see their dragon and mentor. Ruby's family followed quietly behind the twins.

Glisten appeared startled because so many people were around her. The twins spoke with her and calmed her. Lucy, Carter, Jonah, William, Ruby, and Mariposa headed back to Mariposa's home, a yurt.

The twins enjoyed some time alone with Glisten.

Surrounding the yurt were Mariposa's talented neighbors. The Henleys were doctors. The Millers were herp (reptile) veterinarians. The Allens were builders and trackers. Everyone had a deep respect for Mariposa. The couples sensed Glisten might be lonely for her own kind, since no dragons lived in the Wolf Bay area.

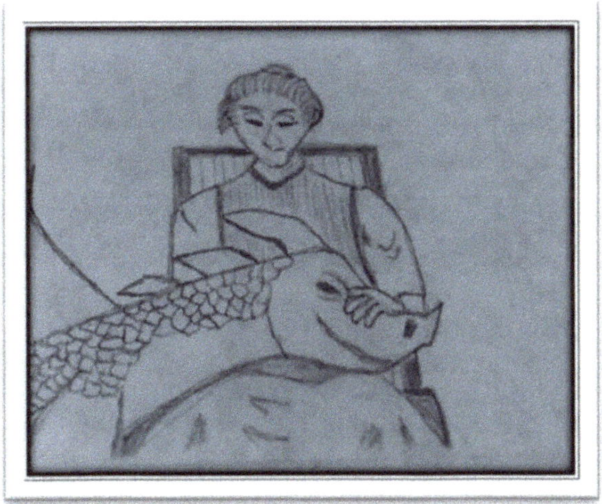

The nine adults formulated a plan
to search for a dragon community.
Mariposa suggested two areas
within the Perdido River estuarine
system: the land around Reeder
Lake and the land between
Threemile Creek and the
Blackwater River, northeast of
Elberta. Like the areas around
Week's Bay and Wolf Bay, these
two estuarine areas were largely
uninhabited.

There were three groups which included Purple Group (health): the Henleys, Jonah, Katarina, and Lucy; Orange Group (trackers): the Allens, William, Carter, and Ruby; and Blue Group (animal care): the Millers, Mariposa, and Kaleb. The teens supervised the preparations for three days of exploring.

Purple Group and **Orange Group** drove as close to the designated areas as possible. They hiked the rest of the way through sandy wiregrass, soil bogs, and marshy wooded swamps. **Blue Group** stayed behind to take care of Glisten and the Wolf Bay properties.

After two days of searching, Purple Group could not find any signs of dragons and decided to head to Orange Group, who were in the Reeder Lake area. On the third day of exploring, the Henleys saw two dragons. The couple ran quickly and quietly back to the groups. William and Jonah noted the location on their maps and the groups returned to Blue Group.

The night of the return, Lucy and Katarina prepared a celebration. The exhausted hikers enjoyed themselves, even after three days of difficult travel. The Henleys suggested everyone rest for at least a day before heading out again. Mariposa recommended Kaleb ride out alone with Glisten while the others hiked to the dragons' home.

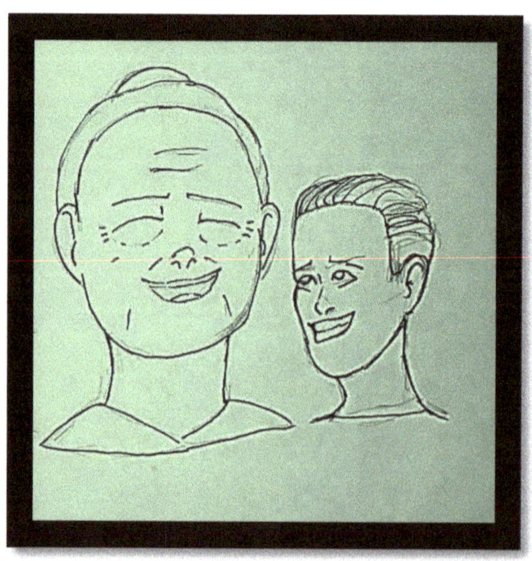

On the day of Glisten's flight to meet the dragons, Kaleb could hardly contain his excitement. Because the Millers worked with groups of large reptiles, they gave Kaleb advice on how to behave around several dragons. William gave Kaleb an updated map.

Kaleb and his dragon took off
early in the morning. It took about
an hour to find the other dragons,
who were resting southwest of
Reeder Lake. Glisten and Kaleb
flew over the dragons to get their
attention. Glisten seemed thrilled
to find her own kind. The dragons
watched cautiously, perhaps
because Glisten had a rider.

Kaleb dismounted Glisten so she could meet the other dragons alone. However, Kaleb stayed hidden nearby in case the situation became dangerous to friendly Glisten. Kaleb listened as the dragons communicated. Fortunately, the dragons were approachable.

William decided his family would return to the Week's Bay farms to take care of the properties and animals. The Henleys and Allens went with William to help out. Blue Group (Millers, Kaleb, and Mariposa) plus Katarina stayed at Wolf Bay.

 and Katarina visited the dragon community often. While with the dragons, Glisten helped her new friends interact with the humans. As veterinarians, the Millers knew they would need to gain the confidence of the dragons before they could care for them.

Although the twins wanted to stay by the dragons, Mariposa needed to bring them back to Ruby's home school for their education. Mariposa used the Millers' vehicle, since the Millers stayed by Reeder Lake to study the dragons' language and care for them.

When Kaleb, Katarina, and Jonah graduated from high school, they wanted to live with Mariposa and the dragons. Kaleb, Jonah, Carter, Lucy, and Katarina named the dragon community Thunder (a group of dragons) Fenland (a wetland).

Mariposa bought land by Thunder Fenland soon after the dragon discovery. After Carter and Lucy graduated from high school, William and Ruby decided to sell both farms and buy land by Mariposa.

Glisten loved living in Thunder Fenland with the other dragons. She seemed thrilled to finally use dragon language again. On the weekends, Kaleb taught Carter how to fly Glisten in the mornings and Katarina taught Lucy in the afternoons.

Glisten selected a strong but quiet mate. Carter, Jonah, and Kaleb named him Ember because he was blue with orange and red hues throughout his body. The warm colors reminded the boys of glowing embers. Glisten encouraged Ember to allow humans to ride him as well.

The following spring, Glisten gave birth to twins, a rare occurrence among dragons. With Mariposa's permission, the Millers lived on her land. In this way, the couple could continue to provide healthcare to the dragons, especially the adorable hatchling twins.

The search for Glisten and others
in her species ended joyfully for
both dragons and people. Kaleb
and Katarina were content as they
entered adulthood; however, they
still wanted to find Glisten's
mother. In fact, they hoped to find
Glisten's parents together like
Glisten and Ember, forever in love.

www.ingramcontent.com/pod-product-compliance
Lightning Source LLC
Chambersburg PA
CBHW050441200726
48295CB00024B/937